minedition

North American edition published 2015 by Michael Neugebauer Publishing Ltd. Hong Kong

Illustrations Copyright © 2015 by Jonas Lauströuer
Rights arranged with "minedition" Rights and Licensing AG, Zurich, Switzerland.
Michael Neugebauer Publishing Ltd., Unit 23, 7F, Kowloon Bay Industrial Centre,
15 Wang Hoi Road, Kowloon Bay, Hong Kong. e-mail: info@minedition.com
This book was printed in July 2015 at L.Rex Printing Co Ltd.,
3/F., Blue Box Factory Building, 25 Hing Wo Street, Tin Wan, Aberdeen, Hong Kong, China
Typesetting in Baskerville Old Face.
Library of Congress Cataloging-in-Publication Data available upon request.

ISBN 978-988-8240-40-1 (US)
ISBN 978-988-8240-34-0 (GB)

10 9 8 7 6 5 4 3 2 1
First Impression

For more information please visit our website: www.minedition.com

The Brothers Grimm
The Hare and the Hedgehog

Pictures by Jonas Lauströer

minedition

This story, my dear young ones, may seem false, but it really is true–for my grandfather, from whom I learned it, always used to say, "It must be true, or else no one could tell it to you." Well, one Sunday morning around harvest time, just when the buckwheat was in bloom, the sun was shining brightly, the morning wind was blowing warmly, the larks were singing, the bees were buzzing, people were dressed in their Sunday best, and all the creatures were happy–including the hedgehog.

The hedgehog stood before his door with his arms crossed, humming a little song to himself, which was neither better nor worse than the songs which hedgehogs are in the habit of singing on a Sunday morning. While he was singing to himself, it suddenly occurred to him that while his wife was bathing the children, he could take a little walk into the field to see how his turnips were doing. The turnips were close by, and as he and his family often ate them, he considered them his own.

The hedgehog shut the door behind him and took the path to the field. He had not gone very far from home, and was just rounding the blackthorn bush which stands at the edge of the field, when he spied the hare who had gone out on business of the same kind–namely, to visit his cabbages.

When the hedgehog caught sight of the hare, he said a friendly good morning. But the hare, who was in his own way a distinguished gentleman, and terribly snooty, did not return the hedgehog's greeting, but said to him in a very disapproving manner, "How do you happen to be running about here in the field so early in the morning?"

"I am taking a walk," said the hedgehog.

"A walk!" said the hare, with a grin.

"It seems to me that you might use your legs for a better purpose."

This answer made the hedgehog furious, for he could stand just about anything but an attack on his legs, which were crooked by nature. So now the hedgehog said to the hare, "You seem to imagine that you can do more with your legs than I can with mine."

"That is just what I think," said the hare.

"We can put that to the test," said the
hedgehog. "I wager that if we run a race,
I will outrun you."

"That's ridiculous! You with your short
legs!" said the hare, "But for my part
I am willing if you are. What shall we
wager?"

"A golden coin and a bottle of mead,"
said the hedgehog.

"Done," said the hare.

"Let's shake hands on it, and then we may
as well take off at once!"

"Not quite yet," said the hedgehog, "I haven't eaten yet. I will go home and have a little breakfast first. In half an hour I will come back again."

On his way back home the hedgehog thought to himself, "The hare relies on his long legs, but I will get the better of him. He may think he is great, but he's foolish, and he'll pay for what he said."

So when the hedgehog reached home, he told his wife, "Dress quickly, you must go out to the field with me."

"What is going on, then?" she asked.

"I have made a wager with the hare for a gold coin and a bottle of mead," the hedgehog said. "I am to run a race with him, and you must be there."

"Good heavens, husband!" his wife cried. "Have you completely lost your wits? What can make you want to run a race with the hare?"

"Wait," said the hedgehog, "don't worry yourself. I have a plan."

What could the hedgehog's wife do? She decided to follow him up to the field to see what would happen.

On the way back to the field, the hedgehog said to his wife, "Now pay attention to my plan. You see, the long field will be our race course. The hare will run in one furrow, and I will run in another, and we will start at the top. All you need to do is to wait down here in the furrow at the bottom, and when the hare arrives, cry out to him, 'I am here already!'"

Then the hedgehog showed his wife where to hide, and started walking up the field. When he reached the top, the hare was already there.

"Shall we start?" said the hare.

"Certainly," said the hedgehog.
As each of them placed himself in his
own furrow, the hare counted, "One,
two, three, and away!"–and he took off
like a whirlwind down the field.
The hedgehog, however, only ran about
three paces, and then he stooped down
in his furrow, and remained quietly
where he was.

When the hare arrived at full speed at the lower end of the field, the hedgehog's wife met him with the cry, "I am here already!"

The hare was shocked. He thought it was the hedgehog himself, for the hedgehog's wife looked exactly like her husband. The hare, however, thought to himself, "That can't be right," and he shouted, "It must be run again, let's run it again!"

And once more he took off like the wind in a storm, so that he seemed to fly. But the hedgehog's wife stayed quietly in her spot. So when the hare reached the top of the field, the hedgehog himself cried out to him, "I am here already!"

The hare was beside himself with anger, and cried, "It must be run again, we must race again!"

"All right," answered the hedgehog, "we'll run as many times as you choose."

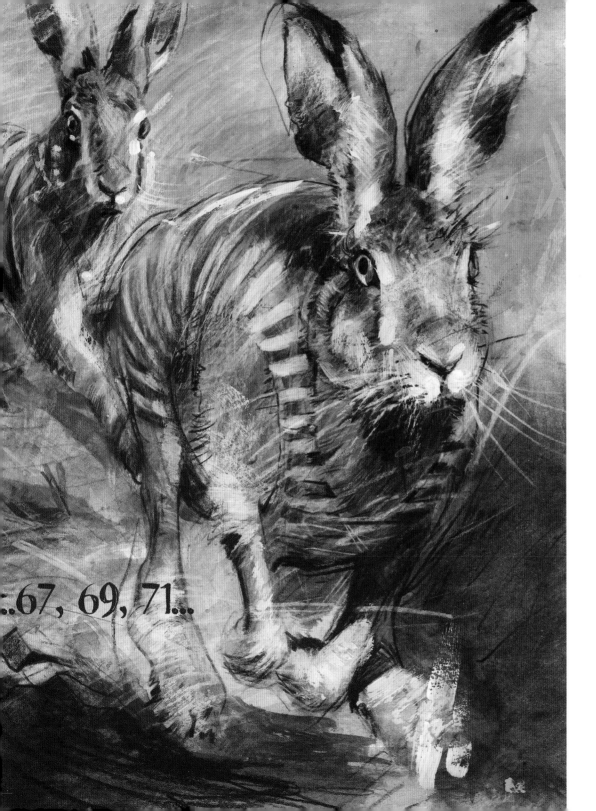

..67, 69, 71...

So the hare ran seventy-three more times, and every time he reached the top or the bottom of the field, either the hedgehog or his wife said, "I am here already!"

The seventy-fourth time, however, the hare could run no longer. In the middle of the field he fell to the ground and lay dead on the spot. The hedgehog took the gold coin and the bottle of mead he had won, called his wife out of the furrow, and they both went home in great delight. And for all I know they are living there still.

That's how the hedgehog made the hare run so many races that he expired, and since then no hare has ever had a notion of running a race with a hedgehog.

The moral of the story is, firstly, that no one—however great he may be, should tease anyone he thinks is beneath him—even if he's only a hedgehog. And, secondly, where fooling others is concerned, it helps to have a partner who can pass as your twin.